Free Agent

Roz Lee

ISBN: 979-8-9917520-2-2
State of Mind Publishing

FREE AGENT

The stress of opening her specialty bakery has kept Brooke tied up in knots, just not the kind she would prefer. When she spies the hunk of a Dom across the crowded bar, she's intrigued, but his wristband shows he's off limits. That doesn't stop her from doing the most daring thing she's ever done to snag a man's attention, but when things escalate beyond even her wildest imaginings, she can't get out of there fast enough.

His contract with the Mustangs expires at the end of the season, and third baseman Todd Stevens is holding out for a longer, more lucrative deal as a free agent. Convinced more money and a new city will cure what ails him, he isn't looking for a long-term relationship, much less a onetime hookup with a sub who doesn't know her place. Unfortunately, the little minx eyeing him from across the room might just be the one to make him change his mind.

AUTHOR'S NOTE

I wrote Free Agent because a wonderful reader expressed interest in knowing more about the secondary characters in Going Deep, the second book of the Mustangs Baseball series. This story takes place before the first book in the series, Inside Heat, and explains how Brooke and Todd met. I hope you enjoy this prequel to the series as much as I enjoyed writing it.

.

CHAPTER ONE

There were only a few sounds Todd Stevens truly loved: the soft shush of a flogger connecting with flesh, the cry a woman makes when she comes, and the solid *thwack* of leather and wood colliding in perfect disharmony.

The first made his dick hard, the second melted his heart, and the third brought a smile to his face.

Todd rounded first base, his lips curving upward as the baseball soared into the centerfield stands. He stepped on second base, vaguely aware of fans scrambling to see who would come up with the homerun ball. Rounding third, his smile faded, even though the entire Mustangs team waited just beyond home plate to celebrate his ninth-inning, game-winning homer.

High-fiving his teammates, he accepted their jubilant accolades, removed his batting helmet, and waved to the crowd before ducking his six-foot-two frame into the dugout that had been his home for his entire Major League career. Thinking about the yet-to-be-determined dugout he would call home next season made his stomach cramp. Less than twenty-four hours ago, he told the Mustangs team management he couldn't accept the contract they'd offered, choosing instead to become a free agent at the conclusion of the season.

Greener pastures were out there, his agent had assured him. Pastures covered in guaranteed green—of the cold, hard cash variety—just waiting for him to sign on the dotted line. At thirty-two years old, the five-year contract the Mustangs offered wasn't bad, but according to his agent, Todd could get a more lucrative seven-year contract with another team and, with the added cash, could retire in style at the ripe old age of thirty-nine.

He wasn't sure if it was the greener pastures beckoning or the change of scenery in general, but over the last year or two, he'd grown increasingly restless. Dallas was home, and he'd made friends here. The media had grown accustomed to him, so they pretty much left him alone off the field, which gave him the freedom to pursue the private lifestyle that had become essential to his existence.

"Hey, Stevens." Tanner Haversford, the Mustangs shortstop, slapped him on the back.

"Hey, yourself." He grabbed his suit coat off the rack in his locker. "What's up?"

"Some of us are going out for drinks. Thought you might want to come along and celebrate the win."

Slipping his arms into his jacket, he declined. "Thanks. I appreciate the offer, but I think I'm going to go on home. That homerun took the last of my wind."

"I hear you, old man," the relative youngster laughed. "I thought that one was going to clear the scoreboard."

He chuckled. "That would have been something to see." He looked around, satisfied he had everything, and headed out.

Tanner fell in step beside him. "One of these days. Either you or Jason Holder are going to at least knock a few light bulbs out."

"Maybe," he hedged.

Six years his junior, Jason Holder was the Mustangs' catcher. He reminded Todd of himself at that age—quiet, confident, and determined to make his mark on the sport. He had no doubt the kid would. It was a shame he wouldn't be around to see it. Another band of regret wrapped around his heart.

"You sure you don't want to come?" They'd made it to the team parking lot where only a few cars remained. "We were hoping we could talk some sense into you, get you to stay."

Well, shit. He should have known. The only things that traveled faster than a homerun ball in the Major League were news and rumors. It was anyone's guess which one of the two held the record. In his case, news was the winner.

He shook his head. "I appreciate it. I really do, but my mind is made up. This is my last season with the Mustangs."

"Okay, then. But I want a rain check on talking sense into you. Another time?"

"Yeah, why not?" He waved goodbye and settled into his car. Leaving these guys would be harder than he thought, but he had to be realistic. Even if the Mustangs could afford to offer him the kind of contract his agent said he deserved, he couldn't stay.

There was something missing in his life, and whatever it was, it wasn't in Dallas. He knew, because he had looked.

Just like you've searched in a dozen other cities the Mustangs have played in. So, what makes you think it will be different somewhere else?

It had to be. There wasn't any other choice. He couldn't go on like this, only feeling alive when he was on the field. Even the lure of a willing sub wasn't cutting it these days. He had a reputation at the Dungeon for being an attentive Dom, and any number of unattached subs would drop to their knees for him.

Only, he hadn't been to the Dungeon in weeks. Just couldn't bring himself to go. And that wasn't like him at all.

He dropped his keys on the hallway table and headed straight for the refrigerator. Beer in hand, he stepped outside to enjoy the quiet night. He'd spent a shitload of money on the pool and landscaping two years ago because he could no longer stand the confines of the house. He owned a five thousand square foot hotel room with a gourmet kitchen. He kept beer in the refrigerator, clothes in the closet in the master bedroom, and the necessities of life in the bathroom. During the season, he kept an open suitcase on the stool at the foot of the bed—the stool he'd originally purchased with the vision of binding the woman of his choice to and fucking her brains out.

But he'd never found that woman.

In the eight years he'd lived in the house, he'd never brought a woman home. At first, he'd liked it that way. Go to the club, find a woman who craved the things he needed to give her—a little pain and a good fuck. Enjoy. No muss. No fuss. Everyone goes home happy.

He couldn't remember the last time he was truly happy—outside of baseball. Nothing had changed there. He still loved the game, craved the rush of pitting his mind and body against the best athletes in the sport.

He was at the top of his game, in his prime—his agent had said. No reason not to put himself on the auction block at the end of the season. There were teams with deep pockets looking for players like him. Players who had the goods, offensively and defensively.

Todd tossed his empty beer bottle in the

waste can and opened the refrigerator in the outdoor bar, in search of another. Finding the small box empty, he cursed, made a mental note to remind his housekeeper to restock that one first, and headed back to the kitchen. Once inside, he suddenly craved something salty to go with his beer and opened the pantry on the off chance there was something to eat. He found an open bag of pretzels, noted the expired freshness date, and grabbed a handful anyway. Before he could test their shelf life, his cell phone rang.

"Saved by the bell," he muttered, tossing the ancient snacks back into the bag. He kicked the pantry door shut and fished the phone from his pocket with one hand while he opened the under-sink trash receptacle with the other.

Without checking the caller ID, he hit the answer button. "Hello?"

"Hey. What are you doing tonight?"

Fuck. He recognized Adam's voice and wasn't in any mood for whatever his friend had in mind. They'd met at the Dungeon a few years ago, two single Doms looking to hook up, but on a play-as-you-go basis. They'd been friends ever since, even shared a sub or two.

He hadn't seen his friend for months.

"Just havin' a beer, chillin'," he said.

"Great game today. Your walk-off homer was awesome. You should be out celebrating."

He shrugged and leaned his hip against the counter. "I am celebrating."

"Oh, I get it. You have someone there."

"Nope. Just me." He didn't expect another Dom to understand

"That just isn't right, man. Look, I'm at The Buggy Whip. There's a munch tonight. You should come down, check out the subs. Maybe pick out one or two and go have some fun, celebrate in style."

It wasn't so long ago he would have jumped at the chance to attend a munch, particularly at The Buggy Whip. The western-themed bar appealed to the horse-crazy women in Dallas, but every few months, the place closed early in order to host a gathering for people in the lifestyle. Few knew the owner, a Dallas socialite, was both horse crazy and a Domme.

"I don't think so," he said, turning down his second social invitation of the evening.

"What's up? Word is you haven't been to

the club in ages. And don't tell me it's because you're having too much fun on the road. I know better."

Unfortunately, he was speaking to the one person on the planet who did know better. Todd had made the mistake of telling his friend about his lack of enthusiasm for just about everything, including sampling the variety of subs to be found in clubs around the country.

"I'm not in the mood, that's all."

"Get. The. Fuck. Down. Here."

He held the phone away from his ear to avoid damage to his eardrum while Adam ranted.

"I won't take no for an answer. You've got to get out, man. Just come down and have a drink. You don't have to hook up. Just see what's on the market. Besides, you know Cassandra saves her best culinary creations for this crowd."

His stomach growled at the mention of the fabulous foods The Buggy Whip's owner provided. Remembering the petrified pretzels he'd almost eaten, he gave in.

"Okay. I'll come. Give me a few minutes to change clothes."

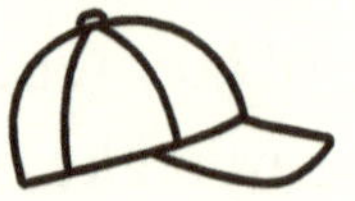

CHAPTER TWO

Wasting my time.

Brooke leaned one elbow on the high top and pretended an interest in the conversation swirling around her. This munch, like all the others she'd been to in the last few months, was getting her nowhere.

It didn't help she was dead on her feet after a full day of work. One of her front counter people had taken a sick day, so she'd done double duty—baking in the pre-dawn hours then helping at the counter during the rush times. In between, she'd finished two wedding cakes due for delivery the next day.

Exhaustion aside, she wouldn't change a thing about her job. Getting her specialty bakery up and running had claimed most of her time and focus for the last year and a half, but all her hard work was paying off. Baked by Brooke had gained a loyal following, and the future looked bright.

She wished she could say the same for her love life. Make that her *non-existent* love life.

It had been way too long since she'd felt the stirring of desire, the inexplicable need to give herself completely to someone. Constant work could do that to a person, she supposed. But something had drawn her to The Buggy Whip tonight, and fatigue aside, she had caved to the impulse. Her feet hurt and the strain of trying to follow a conversation when she wasn't really interested in the subject was beginning to give her a headache.

Abandoning pretense, she let her gaze drift around the room. There was the usual mix of unattached Doms and subs engaged in the tedious job of sizing each other up in the hopes of finding a suitable partner for the rest of the night or longer. Her eyes locked with a familiar set across the room. If she'd had any inclination to submit to the man, she would have looked away, but she held his gaze until he silently acknowledged her with a slight nod, his lips quirking up on one side.

What had it been? Two years? No, more

like three. She and Damon had explored the possibility of a match, but after a few sessions, both agreed to go their separate ways. He hadn't been cruel, but they'd both been searching for something and hadn't found it in each other.

His gaze slid away, and the tension in her stomach eased. *Not even tempted.* That was a good thing. There was no use in going backward, making the same mistakes again. Part of the reason she'd devoted so much time to the startup of her business was to forget the twisted mind-fucks Damon had subjected her to. It hadn't taken long for her to decide she wasn't ready, might never be ready, for his particular brand of domination.

But, here she was again, letting the grip of need drag her into the path of people like Damon.

She shifted her feet and raised her drink to her lips. Ice cubes clinked against the glass when she tipped the cool liquid into her mouth. The red paper bracelet identifying her as a sub seeking a Dom slid down her arm. Placing the glass back on the table, she adjusted the band, almost wishing she hadn't given in and accepted it. At the door, everyone was asked to select a color-coded bracelet. Tonight, green and blue indicated Doms who were and were not seeking subs, red and orange were for the subs.

Discreetly eyeing the male population for a green band attached to an interesting body, she wasn't prepared for the jolt that rocked her back on her heels. He stood in profile, leaning against the bar, talking to another Dom. The first thing she noticed was his hand. Strong fingers held a tumbler filled with dark liquid, which he lifted to his lips. She was so mesmerized by the fullness and shape of those lips she almost missed the flash of blue at his wrist. Damn. He wasn't shopping for a sub.

Just my fucked up luck.

She glanced away, noticed the green band on the wrist of his friend, but felt nothing. Not even a twinge of interest. Blue wristband gestured with his hand, drawing her attention back to him. She straightened her shoulders, thrusting her best assets out. Her skin felt electrified, and her core was well on its way to a meltdown, and all she'd done was look at the man. In profile, no less.

He appeared to be a few years older than her, but his tight jeans and tailored shirt testified to his excellent condition. Firm. Muscular. Broad-shouldered and slim-hipped. She wished he would turn, so she could see his package—gauge the size. It had to be massive. No one that big would have a little cock. God couldn't be so sadistic.

His hair was neatly styled but, at the same time, disheveled as if he knew he was supposed to groom but didn't give a fuck one way or the other. Not a pretty boy who couldn't drag himself away from a mirror.

A faint hint of dark stubble lined his cheek and jaw—not the trendy see-how-much-testosterone-I-have kind, but the damn, I-forgot-to-shave kind. The kind that would abrade a woman's skin, leave a mark to remind her who had claimed her.

Brooke licked her lips and clenched her thighs together as a feeling she thought long forgotten built between her legs. She imagined his cheeks between her legs and his mouth on her pussy. Was he the kind who would restrain her and then take what he wanted?

Hell, yes. He'd do all kinds of things to her, and she wanted every one of them.

Her nipples chafed against the lace edging of her corset, aching for his attention.

She studied the one hand she could see. Clean, neat nails and blunt fingertips. It was a workingman's hand, capable of tenderness when called for yet able to discipline and arouse.

She closed her eyes, imagining him taking the weight of her breasts in his hands, his fingers pinching and tugging on her nipples, his tongue tasting. A bolt of pure lust shot from her breasts to her pussy. Her eyes popped open, and she glanced, looking around, making sure the sound she'd heard in her head hadn't escaped her mouth.

Relief flooded her. None of the others sharing her table seemed to have heard or noticed she was on the sharp edge of coming.

She lifted her drink, took a quick sip, and set the glass down before it shook right out of her hands. What was happening to her? It had clearly been way too long since she'd had a good fuck if she was getting herself off just by imagining a guy touching her. Hell, she hadn't even touched herself. How pathetic was that?

"Penny for your thoughts." The words, spoken in a low voice next to her ear startled her half out of her skin. She turned to the friend who had encouraged her to attend the munch.

"Karen. You scared me."

"That's because you were off in sub-space somewhere. What's up with that? Did you let some Dom wire you with a remote vibrator or something and not tell me?"

Brooke clamped the edge of the table to steady herself. Her friend was right. She'd been in sub-space, and she'd gotten there all by herself. Her skin still tingled with arousal and a desperate need to feel his hands on her, but he wasn't available tonight. She needed to get a grip.

"No. I…I was…."

"Don't tell me you were daydreaming. I'm not going to buy it. Your skin is flushed, and your eyes are glazed. What are you drinking?" She grabbed Brooke's drink and sniffed. One eyebrow rose. "Soda?"

"Diet. No alcohol. I'm not stupid. You know I make lousy decisions when I drink." *Damon.*

"Then what's going on? No alcohol. No vibrator. Who's got you so worked up?"

"It doesn't matter. He's not looking tonight." She tapped her own red bracelet. "Blue."

Karen surveyed the room. "Which one? Are you sure?"

"I'm sure." She wasn't about to tell her friend which man it was. A woman was entitled to her private fantasies.

"I only see one."

Brooke followed the direction of her cohort's gaze, and her breath caught in her throat.

"He's looking at you."

"No shit, Sherlock." His gaze held hers for a breath-stealing minute, then slowly descended to her breasts. Released from the strength of his stare, she focused on the hand holding a tumbler at his chest. He brought the glass to his lips.

Without thinking, her hand dropped to the juncture of her thighs, her middle finger finding her swollen clit. Seeing her movement, he leaned a little to one side.

She didn't know what made her do it. Her finger brushed her clit once. Twice. Again. She tumbled over the edge. Spasms racked her body, her pussy clenching so hard the muscles in her abdomen felt like someone had taken a cattle prod to them. She bit her bottom lip to hold in the cries choking her vocal cords. With her free hand, she held onto the edge of the table, a tiny scrap of sanity in the chaos enveloping her body.

"He might not be looking, but he's definitely *looking*," Karen said, turning back, undoubtedly to offer more words of unwanted encouragement. She reached out, grabbing Brooke by both arms, supporting her before her knees buckled. "Did you just come?" Her eyes were wide with disbelief. "You just came! Oh my God!"

"No."

"Don't even try to deny it. Girl, if you don't introduce yourself to him, blue band or not, you're going to regret it for the rest of your life."

"I can't."

"Yes, you can."

She took a deep breath and let it out before downing the rest of her soda in one long gulp. Good thing she hadn't had anything stronger or no telling what she might have done. Strip naked and walk across the room to offer herself to him. Yeah, that sounded right. She wasn't sure what she'd actually done had been any less revealing or humiliating.

"What's he doing?" she asked, not daring

to look his way again.

"He just ordered another drink. Telling, don't you think?"

"No." She couldn't allow herself to think her shameless act had affected him anywhere near as much as it had her. "I'm so embarrassed. I can't believe I just did that."

"He is gorgeous, isn't he? Do you know him?"

"Never saw him before."

"But you'd get on your knees for him if he asked."

She confessed her earlier thoughts about stripping naked in the middle of the room for him. "Yeah. But blue. Remember?"

"Maybe he just didn't want to be bothered by every sub in the place tonight. He sure seemed interested in your little *performance*."

Brooke buried her face in her hands. "Half the people in here probably saw that."

"Half is probably being too generous. Maybe twenty-five percent."

"Ugh!"

"Look. What have you got to lose? Go over there, say hello, drop your gaze and see if he takes the lead. If not, then you might as well go on home. There isn't a Dom in here who would take what they think is clearly his. Not without an invitation, at least."

She hadn't thought of that. The BDSM crowd had rules, and poaching was high on the list of *don'ts*. To the rest of the group, it must have looked as if she was his and they were playing some sort of private game with each other—a bar pickup or come-in-public challenge. Her friend was right. There wasn't another Dom in the bar who would approach her.

"I'm going home," she said.

"You've got to go past him to get to the door." Her grin was wicked. "What have you got to lose? Stop and introduce yourself."

"I can't. God, isn't there another way out of this place?"

"Nope. Cassandra doesn't let people go through the kitchen unless it's an emergency."

If her predicament wasn't an emergency, she didn't know what was. She stopped short of voicing the thought, sighing instead. "I'll see you soon. I'll get out of your way so you can find someone. Maybe his friend?"

Karen glanced at the two men still talking at the bar. "Maybe. He's hot, too."

"I suppose."

"Girl, you've got it bad. Go on, now. Scoot on out of here before you make yourself come again. How embarrassing would that be?"

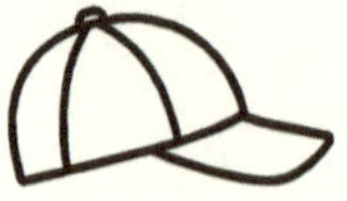

CHAPTER THREE

Todd signaled the bartender for another soda. He needed something cold to send down his gullet to put out the fire raging inside him, and he needed a few seconds to decide what to do next.

He'd sensed her gaze on him a while ago, but since he wasn't at The Buggy Whip to pick up anyone, he'd resisted the urge to look. He was used to being stared at, assessed. It usually didn't bother him, but for some reason tonight, he felt this person's scrutiny all the way down to his toes. Hell, he'd been half-hard before he finally gave in and glanced around, cautiously. He had no intention of encouraging her. He wasn't about to get involved with a woman—not when he wouldn't be sticking around for the long haul—and one-night stands didn't hold the appeal they once did.

He singled her out just as she turned back to face the others at her table, giving him an opportunity to return the favor of cataloging her assets.

She was stunning. A corset and short skirt hugged rather than defined her shapely petite frame. Honey-blonde hair hung in soft waves over bare shoulders, framing fine features, porcelain fair skin, and blue eyes. A red bracelet indicated she was available. Deciding he liked the package, he waited to see if she would check him out again.

She glanced at the woman beside her then nervously, he thought, her attention darted back to him. For a moment, he was unable to look away. It was as if she saw past his defenses, right to his soul.

Fuck. He'd never had fanciful thoughts, so why was he now? He jerked his gaze down to her breasts. His skin did that thing again, prickling wherever she looked. She seemed fixated on his hand, so he raised his glass to his lips and drank.

Her arm dropped to her side. A zing of electricity ran from his nape all the way to his balls. *What the fuck was she doing?* Leaning to one side, he watched, completely and utterly fascinated, as her middle finger toyed with a spot she had no business touching without permission from someone.

He leaned heavier on the bar, clutching the cool glass in one hand, contracting the other into a tight fist. It took all of thirty seconds, perhaps less, before she came. Right there in the bar. God, he'd never seen anything like it. Anger, hot and surprisingly violent, shot through him. He turned away, threw the remainder of his soda down his throat in one gulp, and ordered another.

What had the little cunt been thinking? He wasn't looking for companionship, but she clearly had other ideas. He should lay her out on the bar, hike her skirt up to her waist, and paddle her ass until she came again. He'd teach her to top from the bottom.

"You okay?" Adam asked.

"Yeah, just fucking fine." He leaned both forearms on the bar and stared into his refilled glass. "Tell me you didn't set this up."

"Hey," his friend laughed. "I wish I'd

thought of it, but no. It's just your lucky night, I guess.

"Lucky night, my ass. I shouldn't have come here."

"Well, you did, and if you don't take her out of here, there are half a dozen other tops who will. They're waiting to see what you're going to do. I'm guessing most of them think she's yours, and this is some sort of scene you set up for her. The rest are praying it isn't and that they have a chance with her. I'm in the last bunch."

He clenched his jaw tight and said through stiff lips, "Don't fucking touch her, or I'll twist your dick off."

The other Dom had the balls to chuckle. "Hey, man. I don't poach. Can't vouch for the rest of them."

"I don't want her." He hated the way the lie felt like a hot poker stabbing his heart. His cock was so hard he couldn't think straight.

"Whatever you say." He glanced over his shoulder. "You'd better make up your mind fast. She's leaving."

Oh, hell no, she wasn't leaving. He swung around, prepared to stop her but resisted the urge. She sailed past him in her spike heels, her chin held high. Christ, she was a little thing. She almost looked fragile, but that was an illusion. Any woman who could do what she had just done had to be made of steel. Too bad he wasn't staying around, and because he wasn't, he let her walk out the door.

"And here I thought you were a smart man," Adam said, turning back to the bar once the door closed behind the mystery woman.

"Shut the fuck up."

He couldn't get her out of his mind. Two weeks had gone by since he'd seen her at The Buggy Whip, and he'd come to the Dungeon every night the team had been in town since in a futile attempt to find her. Why hadn't he asked her name? She'd been with friends; he was sure of it, but it had been a matter of pride. He didn't want to admit he'd made a mistake letting her walk out alone, and he sure as hell didn't want the other Doms in the place knowing she wasn't his just in case they found her before he did.

Funny, he couldn't remember seeing any of her friends from the munch at the Dungeon either. That meant they all played on the fringes, at home, among themselves, or they frequented one of the other clubs in the area.

He was shit out of luck if either of those were the case. If they played within an insular group, he'd never find her, and he couldn't very well go traipsing around to the other clubs. People knew and respected him at the Dungeon. He trusted them to keep his involvement in the lifestyle to themselves. He couldn't expect the same discretion from a place he didn't know. He couldn't risk it. Being well-known around town had its drawbacks for people with needs like his.

"I thought you weren't interested in casual pickups anymore." Adam joined Todd at the small table in the social area where he'd set up his casual surveillance.

At one time or another, nearly everyone in the Dungeon came through the space to grab a water bottle or meet friends. It was where the unattached hung out looking for action. She'd been looking for action then, so it stood to reason he'd find her here. If she came.

"I'm not."

His companion crossed his arms on the table and scanned the crowd. "Looking for anyone in particular?"

"I just said I'm not looking for anyone."

"But that was a lie. I know you. She got to you. You should have stopped her before she left that night and put a collar on her."

Fuck, yeah. On the field, indecision was the enemy. A player had split seconds, at best, to make a decision and commit to a plan of action if he hoped to have any success at all. The same applied to being a Dom.

He'd known when he saw her he had to have her, but he'd been trying to do the right thing and not start something he would have to end—probably before either one of them was ready for it to end. What was the saying? Nice guys finish last. Or not at all. He'd turned down every sub who had looked his way since she'd walked out of the bar because none of them had been her.

"I fucked up," he admitted, focusing on the tepid water bottle he'd been hanging onto all evening like a buoy.

"If you had a second chance, would you take it?"

He nodded. "Yeah. I would. All I've been able to think about is paddling her ass and showing her how much better it is with my dick inside her."

"Don't look now, buddy, but you might get to do those things after all."

"What?" He jerked his head up, his gaze automatically going to the doorway. His heart could power half the city it was racing so fast.

"That's her, isn't it?"

"That's her."

A red lace thing—nothing more than a wide band—hugged her every curve like an expensive sports car on a mountain road. From the looks of it, she didn't have a stitch on underneath.

"You going to go get her?"

God, he wanted to, but for some perverse reason, he needed her to come to him. He forced his gaze back to his water bottle. "Not yet. Let's see what she does. She might be with someone."

The pushy bastard leaned down, got in his face. "Have you lost your mind?" he asked in a tight-lipped growl meant only for Todd's ears. "Go get her. Now. Before someone else does."

He shook his head. "Give her a few minutes. She'll come to me." He raised his head, following her movement. She crossed the room to another table where a couple of subs for the taking had set up shop, hoping for a chance to play. He knew two of the other three—he'd spent a few pleasurable hours with each of them, maybe more than once.

"She's talking to Candy."

"I see that," he growled.

The two women had their heads together, talking. Candy shifted her eyes, looking directly at him. She was perceptive, which made her an excellent sub. He inclined his head in a silent signal she was sure to understand. Her lips curved up on one side, and she winked at him before returning her attention to the woman in red.

The two consorts pushed their chairs back and stood.

"How did you do that?" Adam asked.

"What?"

"Know she would come to you. Get both of them to come to you."

He shrugged. "I have no idea. I only want the one in red. You can have Candy."

"I wasn't going to play tonight."

"Then you can watch me."

"I might just do that."

The two women stopped in front of their table and stood, eyes downcast, waiting to be addressed. His palms itched. He dropped his hands beneath the table and flexed his fingers to keep from reaching for her.

"Candy," he said. "Permission to speak."

"Thank you, sir. I would like to introduce you to a friend of mine, if that pleases you."

"Go ahead."

"Sir, this is Brooke. She has something she wants to tell you."

He refused to smile. It wouldn't do for the minx to see how satisfied he was she had used the proper channels to approach him. She wasn't a habitual rule-breaker, at least. Some subs craved pain so much they went out of their way to break the rules just for the pleasure of being punished. That wasn't his style, but he'd never shied away from punishment when truly warranted. He turned his attention to the woman who had been driving him insane for the last two weeks.

"Permission to speak."

"I've done something naughty, sir, and I need to be punished for it." Her voice was soft, but she spoke boldly.

Christ. His dick nearly leaped right out of his pants. He swallowed hard and reminded himself not to react the way he wanted to because he had a pretty good idea what she would say next. "What did you do?"

"I saw you a few weeks ago at The Buggy Whip, sir. I'm ashamed to tell you, but I must. I should have that night, but I was too embarrassed." She took a deep breath and let it out.

Todd waited while she composed herself. She had to know she was taking a chance asking him to punish her not knowing anything about him, but he wouldn't make it easy for her to confess. She'd been bold enough to commit the offense, so she needed to be bold enough to own up to it. That's the only way they could have any kind of relationship.

"I saw you across the room, sir, and I made myself come."

"You've come here seeking punishment for something you did without my permission?"

"Yes, sir. I should have approached you that night and asked you for permission to come."

"Why didn't you?"

"Your bracelet said you weren't looking. I thought you already had a sub."

"You were right not to approach me

under the circumstances, but you still took matters into your own hands."

"Yes, sir. I was sorry afterward. I knew I had to find you and apologize, and ask you to punish me. I understand if you already have a sub and don't want to bother with me. But, please, I beg you. I need to know you forgive me, so I can move on."

Silence could be as effective as any instrument of pain. He let the moments tick by. She stood her ground, the color leaching from her skin until he judged she understood her latest transgression—topping from the bottom.

"You don't have a master?"

"No, sir."

"Very well, then. I accept your apology, and since it will make you feel better, I'll administer an appropriate punishment. But I'm not looking for a sub. I want you to know that up front. I'll take care of you tonight, but that's all it will be. One night."

She nodded. "Thank you, sir. I understand."

He considered his options. He could modify his bar top fantasy, have her bend over the table, paddle her ass right here, and send her on her way afterward. His body argued against that scenario. If he only had one night with her, it wouldn't be over that fast.

"Candy," he addressed the other sub who remained by her friend's side. "Go up front and see if there's a private room available. Any of them will do. If so, ask them to put it on my tab."

Adam looked at him with raised eyebrows as Candy left on the errand. "Do you know what you're doing?"

"I'm going to punish her so she doesn't forget a sub doesn't own her orgasms. She doesn't choose when or how she will have them."

He had to give her credit. She remained perfectly still, her eyes averted while he discussed her upcoming punishment. Any Dom would admire a package like her, beautiful and disciplined enough to know she'd done something she shouldn't have. That she owned up to it to a stranger either made her brave or stupid. He was inclined to believe the latter.

"Why not a public room? Wouldn't that be more effective?" Adam asked.

"Not for what I have in mind. However,

you're welcome to watch." He would teach this girl a lesson and enjoy every minute of the instruction. He could think of all manner of ways to make her pay for her misbehavior, and every one of them made his cock twitch in anticipation.

"I'll pass, thank you." The other man turned to watch Candy approach. "I think I might enjoy a piece of candy, if I can find one looking to be eaten."

Todd chuckled. "Whatever."

Candy resumed her place beside his new plaything.

"Which room is mine?" he asked her.

"Nine, sir. Will you be needing me, too, sir?"

He noted the hopeful inflection and almost regretted he wasn't interested. Perhaps another time. He couldn't remain celibate for the rest of the season. That wasn't an option.

"No, but Master Adam might be interested."

"I'm in the mood for dessert," The other Dom addressed Candy. "I'll see you receive a treat, too, if you would like to join me."

Her shoulders had slumped ever so slightly at his rejection, but returned to a more confident pose when he issued the invitation. She wouldn't be disappointed tonight. His friend knew what he was doing. He'd treat her right.

Todd stood. With a nod to his friend, he stepped toward Brooke. "Follow me."

CHAPTER FOUR

Her legs felt like jelly, but she wasn't going to back out now. She'd had fourteen days to imagine submitting to this man. Luck was on her side. Word had spread in the sub community she was looking for a particular Dom, and finally, Candy had heard. If she'd called any earlier, Brooke would have chickened out, but with only an hour's notice to meet at the Dungeon, she'd barely had enough time to shower and pick out something to wear, much less think about what she was about to do.

Still, when she stepped into the social room, it took every ounce of courage she had not to bolt. She didn't even have to look to know he was there. Every fiber of her being knew it. Instead, she'd focused on Candy, a sub she'd met a time or two at a few munches.

He stopped at a closed door. She halted a few feet back and waited.

"Do you still want to do this?" he asked.

"Permission to speak frankly, sir?"

"Granted. What's on your mind?"

"I don't know your name, sir."

"My name is Todd. Is there anything else?"

"No, sir. I just wanted—"

"No problem. You're entitled to that much. Look at me."

Her breath came in short pants, her imagination running a marathon. She looked up. She'd only seen him from across the room a few weeks ago and in her periphery tonight. Confronted with the reality so close, she couldn't believe what she'd done. He was gorgeous. Tall, broad-shouldered, and any woman's dream of masculine perfection, he made her mouth dry and her pussy wet. She clamped her thighs tight, afraid she might do the unforgivable and come in the hallway.

He's going to touch me. "Sir," she said, though her mouth felt like it was stuffed with cotton.

"Once we go inside, you're mine until I tell you otherwise. I intend to punish you for stealing an orgasm that was rightfully mine. Punishment is not intended to be pleasant. It is intended to reinforce the discipline you should have in your life. I think you know that since you came to me, but just in case, I need to know you understand."

"I do, sir. I knew what I was doing was wrong, but I wasn't strong enough to stop. I trust you to help me, so I won't do it again."

"The room is ours for the night. Once the punishment is done, I'll give you the choice to stay and let me guide us both to pleasure or not. You are completely free to choose. I'll respect whatever decision you make."

"Thank you, sir."

"Let's do this, then." He opened the door, motioned her inside.

She glanced around quickly before he shut the door, and she would be required to resume her subservient pose. It was her first time at this club as the membership dues were out of her reach. Now, she understood why. She'd only caught a glimpse of a few public rooms, following a guide to the social area where Candy had instructed her to meet. The public rooms were elaborate and well-appointed. This, however, was beyond anything she had seen.

Several large pieces of apparatus occupied the floor space. Overhead, an extensive track system held a wide array of chains, bars, and pulleys for bondage play. Closed cabinets lined one wall, presumably filled with anything a Dom might need. Her gaze landed on the spanking bench in the center of the room. Medieval in style, it was modern in construction with thick leather-covered pads for a sub's comfort. She immediately assumed he would restrain her there to administer her punishment.

"Lie down on the bed," he said, startling her out of her musing. "Face down. You can take off the shoes, but leave everything else on."

The bed? Her heart pounded. That seemed much more intimate than the spanking bench. Why hadn't she considered he would have his own ideas about how to punish her? For the first time since she'd left The Buggy Whip two weeks ago, she wondered if she'd made a mistake in seeking him out.

"Now." His voice boomed behind her,

spurring her toward the bed. Bracing one hand on the edge, she removed one high-heeled sandal and then the other before crawling on her knees to the center of the bed and lying down.

"Up you go."

A soft whir filled the room, and the bed slowly rose a few feet. Table height, she guessed.

"Arms above your head."

Her breasts squashed painfully into the firm mattress, and it took a few tries to figure out what to do with her face. To the left so she could see him? Or the right? She settled on right and raised her arms. He cuffed her swiftly, drawing the connecting chain tight, restraining her close to the line between comfort and pain.

"Everything you've done so far leads me to believe you've had some experience in the lifestyle and you understand I won't push you beyond what you can stand. But, this is a first for us, so say yellow if you need a minute before we continue, red if you can't take anymore. Do you understand?"

"Yes, sir. Yellow for a break. Red to stop."

"Good girl. Let me adjust the lighting."

He stepped away, the padded flooring muffling his steps. The overhead lights dimmed except for one spotlight glowing approximately above her buttocks. He returned, clamped his fingers around her ankles. She'd felt a little zing when he'd lifted her wrists to attach the cuffs, but this…oh, Lord! Electricity sizzled across her skin all the way to the tips of her ears, and she knew with a certainty she had misjudged this man. He was going to turn her inside out and leave her an empty shell she was afraid no one but he could fill.

He only wants one night.

The word "red" flashed in her brain like an out-of-order traffic signal. She should stop this before it went any further. But his hands were traveling up her legs, not spreading them, just touching, sensitizing her skin to the feel of him. He had the hands of a man who worked hard for a living, callused and rough, yet everywhere he touched he was gentle. It was a potent combination that mollified the panicked voice of reason in her head.

No matter what happened tonight, she wouldn't be the same person tomorrow. He'd already changed her. She was his.

He only wants one night.

"Two weeks ago, I wanted to lay you out on the bar, bare your ass to everyone there, and spank you until you begged me to let you come. You cheated me out of that, too, so tonight I'm going to punish you for both."

His voice was Prozac to her system. She heard his words, felt his hands on her skin, slowly working their way up the back of her thighs. Then they were under the hem of her dress, caressing the bare skin he found there.

"I knew you didn't have anything on under this sorry excuse for a dress." He pushed the fabric to her waist. The air in the room seemed as if it came straight from the Arctic Circle when it met the skin where his hands had been. She squirmed, clenching her cheeks tight when she realized he was looking at her bare ass.

He landed a stinging blow to her right buttock, bringing tears to her eyes. She cried out at the sudden burst of pain.

"Don't move." Chains rattled. He jerked her feet wide, secured them with cuffs at her ankles, so she was open to him. "I like the way my handprint looks on your skin."

He covered the sting with his palm. The heat from his hand went straight to her heart and wrapped it in a blanket of warmth.

"How many times should I spank you for what you did?" He trailed a blunt finger along the tight seam. Her body responded, relaxing, allowing him access to her most secret place. "Tell me what you think. How many times?"

Just touch me, she wanted to say. "As many times as you want, sir. I took too much from you."

"You did at that."

Before she could register the loss of contact, he landed another blow on her left cheek. A whimper escaped her lips, and she just barely resisted the urge to lift her ass to beg for more.

He knew better than not to follow through on his promise to punish her. He gained no satisfaction in marring her perfect ass for that reason alone. He much preferred to tease and tantalize…arouse his sub and himself.

Ten hard swats. After the first four, she quit presenting, begging for him to grant her release, and accepted he really was going to punish her. Her whimpers and moans of satisfaction had changed to muffled cries, and he didn't have to look to know he'd brought tears to her eyes. Some lucky Dom would thank him later for reminding her not to toy with her master.

He left her long enough to wet a towel at the sink in the corner. "You were very brave," he said, returning to place the cool cloth over her red bottom. "Are you okay?"

She sniffled and nodded. As she dragged in a ragged breath, her whole body shook. Todd slipped his hand beneath her dress bunched at the small of her back, stroking slowly. Her skin was warm silk, and her heart beat furiously beneath his palm. After a few minutes, some of the tension left her body, and he relaxed a little, too. She was dealing with the pain in her own way, internalizing the lesson.

"What did you learn?"

Another sniffle. Her lungs inflated, and a breath shuddered out of her. "I learned to ask permission to orgasm, sir."

"And?"

"I learned not to touch myself without permission."

He smiled even though she couldn't see. "Then I have done my job. Is there anything you would like to ask me now?" He let his hand wander the length of her spine, memorizing every inch, every curve. "You can ask for anything you want."

"Would you…touch me, sir? Please?"

He loved the timidity in her voice. She was aware of his strength now, yet she still craved the pleasure he had denied her earlier. Her knowledge of the lifestyle was apparent, but he didn't think she had all that much practical experience. Maybe he would push her just a little before he gave her what they both wanted.

"Touch you how? Where?"

She wiggled her ass. "Please, sir."

"Not until you tell me where. I want to give you exactly what you need, but I can't do that unless you're specific." He lifted the towel and tossed it aside. His palm hovered over her left cheek. The heat was gone, but the color remained. Next time, he'd enjoy putting it there.

What next time? He jerked his hand away before he touched her. No. There was only tonight, and only because he'd had no choice. Her misbehavior had weighed heavily on her, and he would have been a complete ass not to take the worry off her shoulders. But anything else tonight was up to her. She wasn't his, so he wouldn't presume anything.

"Sir?"

"Tell me exactly where you want me to touch you. Honesty is one of the best gifts a sub can give her master."

He waited while she digested his words. She looked like a buffet of sensual delights, lying there trussed and open. Having her covered except for her most vulnerable parts excited him. It was as if they were having an illicit affair in a public place, and if discovery was imminent, he had only to yank her dress back down and no one would be the wiser. Next time, he'd see all of her.

No. No next time.

"Sir, please touch my pussy."

His heart swelled with pride. She was one brave woman, asking for punishment and then for pleasure. With one finger, he swept a lock of her hair behind her ear. "Do you want me to make you come?"

"Yes, sir. Please."

"You have been so good, accepting you punishment with such courage, I can't deny you an orgasm. Let me make it the best you've ever had."

"Yes." No hesitation.

Her trust humbled him. Someone was going to be very lucky to own her completely. Too bad it wasn't going to be him.

Todd located a small pillow and slipped it beneath her pelvis, opening her further to him. For the first time, he looked closely at her pussy. She had trimmed neatly. Her outer lips were swollen and rosy with arousal. Parting them, he sucked in a breath at the loveliness of her vaginal opening. Glossy pink petals framed a perfectly shaped slit. He swiped two fingers through the moisture leaking from her and explored lower. A gasp confirmed he'd found her clitoris.

"You are beautiful. I'm going to take my time. Beauty like this should be savored."

She answered with a groan that sounded like it had begun somewhere near her clit and collected need along the way.

His position, standing over her, allowed him to use both hands at once. With his right, he cupped her mound, pressing her clit into the palm of his hand. He traced her inner lips with the fingers of his left hand, delving closer to the well of heat and the source of the ache driving her to commit the act that had brought them together tonight.

She'd paid for her transgressions, so it was time to give her what she had wanted all along—his touch.

He entered her, his middle finger plunging hard. Her inner walls tightened around him, and her hips lifted, trying to suck him in deeper. He gave her his full length then pulled out before thrusting to his third knuckle once more. Keeping constant pressure on her clit, he sought and found her sweet spot. It didn't take much trial to rub his knuckles over the sensitive nub. Her shoulders rose, and she pressed her face into the mattress.

Strangled sounds of ecstasy met his ears and drove him on. He pushed her beyond her ability to control her body. Her hips moved in rhythm with his thrusts, seeking the pleasure he had promised her.

She was so damned beautiful. Her responses thrilled and excited him. It was as if her body talked to him, telling him exactly how much pressure to apply, where to touch her, how hard to plunge, when she was too close to the edge. He backed off, letting her come down from the peak before driving her to the edge again. He'd heard mountain climbers talk of unsuccessful attempts to reach the peak, but when they finally reached the top, the accomplishment was sweeter because of the other times they'd tried and failed.

Giving her the experience filled him with satisfaction. Nothing in the world felt better than seeing a woman reach the peak and fly— at his command.

Call him a control freak, but yeah, he loved commanding a woman's body, especially one that listened and responded like Brooke's.

She was close. Tension coiled in her body as it had several times before. But this instance was different. She'd forgotten the punishment and had used the lingering pain to fuel her climb to the top. It was time to remind her how she'd gotten this far.

Todd leaned over, opened his mouth against her spread crease, and took her ass in a kiss that demanded her complete attention and total surrender. His tongue flicked over the tight rosebud he'd yet to explore.

She froze beneath him. He scraped his teeth over the tender flesh he'd reddened earlier. At the same moment his hands demanded she leap over the edge.

Her response was the most beautiful thing he'd ever witnessed. The mattress muffled a low, keening moan. Her body quaked and jerked in uninhibited waves of passion that gathered him up and towed him along for the wild ride. His cock throbbed with the need to be inside her, to experience the miracle up close and personal.

Adrenaline flooded his system. Blood rushed south, blinding him, but heightened his other senses, so he wouldn't miss a single moment of her orgasm.

He inhaled deeply, drawing her scent into his nostrils, committing it to memory. He'd never forget the feel of her juices pouring over his hands or the sounds she made when she came, like a symphony written only for him and sweeter than the roar in the stadium when he homered.

And he'd done this, brought her to climax. Nothing on the planet could feel better.

"Thank you, Master."

Nothing but that.

CHAPTER FIVE

Shit.

Todd carefully extracted his fingers from her tight channel and, with as gentle a touch as he could muster, tended to his sub.

She called you Master.

She's not yours. You have to let her go.

He wet a washcloth with warm water and cleansed her. Afterward, he rubbed ointment over the angry red welts on her ass cheeks.

I did that to her. No wonder she called me Master. I behaved like her master would.

Finally, he released her ankles and wrists. She lay quiet while he slid the pillow from beneath her hips and pulled her dress down to cover her.

Silent, he scooped her up and carried her

to the big easy chair in the corner. He spread his legs, suspending her sore bottom in the cradle of his thighs. She clung to him, her arms around his neck, her face in the crook of his shoulder.

She trusted me when she had no reason to.

He cradled her until her breathing fell into the soft rhythm of sleep. Then he held her some more. It felt right.

In all the years he'd been a practicing Dom, he'd never just held a woman like this. No demands. No expectations. Offering comfort and shelter—nothing more.

A feeling he couldn't identify crept over him like a thick fog, obscuring his vision and muting his other senses. It wasn't unpleasant. In fact, it was nice. For once, he wasn't in any hurry to leave.

Contentment?

No. But something close.

Whatever it was, the longer he held her, the stronger the feeling became. And as the minutes passed, he came to one conclusion.

I don't want to let her go.

She was dreaming. Nothing in real life had ever felt this good, this right. Wherever she was, she was safe. If she opened her eyes, the dream would shatter, and she wanted it to go on forever.

Slowly, reality seeped through the ragged seams of her consciousness. *Todd.*

She recognized his scent and the feel of his hands. One curved over her arm, the other at her hip, holding her, protecting her. He could have sent her away afterward, but he hadn't. After the most amazing orgasm of her life, he'd simply picked her up as if she weighed nothing and cradled her in his arms. It was as unexpected as it was comforting, but she'd taken her cues from him and hadn't said a word, hadn't questioned his reasons. His broad chest and strong arms had simply felt too good.

What was it about this man that prompted her to do crazy, reckless things? Like make herself come in a public place then foolishly use every contact she knew to find out who he was? Putting herself at his mercy tonight, without a single concrete reason to believe he wouldn't hurt her—other than the feeling in her gut—had been the definition of insanity.

Yet, here she was, in his arms feeling safer than she ever had in her life.

Master.

The word rolled around in her head like a firecracker dancing with a lit match, ready to explode any minute. A sane person would throw the explosive away before it blew up in their face, but she'd already established her insanity.

He only wants one night.

Master.

That deep down, know-it's-right feeling didn't fit a one-night hookup. The feeling went with forever. She'd never envisioned a lasting relationship with another Dom, much less expressed the desire for such an association. But she'd called *him* Master.

He hadn't acted like he'd heard her, and perhaps he hadn't. Maybe that part had been a dream, and she hadn't said the word out loud, only imagined she had. She tested it again, forming the sounds silently with her lips.

"You're awake." His voice rumbled through his chest cavity like a giant cat purring, and she was suddenly aware he could easily tear her to shreds.

Raising her hand to his chest, she felt his heart beating, slow and steady. No sign he was as nervous as she was. "Yes." *Master.* Her brain automatically tacked on the title though she stopped the sound before it passed her lips.

"It's late."

"I should go," she said, though she made no effort to move, and thankfully, he didn't try to make her. She would have to leave his arms, but a piece of her would remain when she did. He'd claimed a part of her no one else ever had—her heart.

He'd changed her in some fundamental way she didn't fully understand. Before, even up until he'd spanked her a few times, she had expected the punishment to be mild, the pain grease that would open the door to her pleasure. She'd expected him to enjoy punishing her. He'd quickly disabused her of the notion. There hadn't been anything sexual about the spanking, and he hadn't enjoyed it. There'd been no soothing between blows. No words spoken to let her know he was turned on, and the pain had been beyond anything arousing. Her ass still hurt and probably would for days.

Up until then, she'd been a selfish sub. She'd offered herself to Dom's for her pleasure, not theirs. She'd expected Todd to follow suit. Paddle her a little—until she was aroused—then bring her to orgasm.

Now, she understood. The real pleasure came from pleasing her master, not the other way around. She'd deliberately taunted him, using his good looks to help herself to a public orgasm, then blithely assuming he would give her another.

"That wasn't what you thought was going to happen, was it?"

She shook her head. "No."

"Don't expect an apology. You won't get one. One thing you have to remember, always. You're here to serve my pleasure, and only my pleasure. I decide when, or if, you will orgasm."

Her heart lodged in her throat. Was he saying what she thought he was saying?

"I'll draw up a contract tomorrow. You should know up front I'm not staying in Dallas much longer. A few months, but I want you with me until I have to go."

Her heart sank like a stone, landing with a sickening thud in her abdomen. *Not forever. A few months.*

"I'll teach you what you need to know to serve your next master."

Black dots swam around her vision. She closed her eyes to stave off a wave of dizziness.

Next master. Not forever.

Forever.

Forever for her. Even when he's gone.

He shifted, pushed her body off his chest, yet still held her in his lap. "Look at me."

She forced her eyes open and turned her face to his. His wonderfully handsome face was a blur through the tears threatening to spill over.

"Why are you crying?" he asked.

Her heart was a petrified fossil lodged somewhere in her body, but she couldn't tell him how he had wounded her. It would hurt him. She could see it in his eyes, and she couldn't do that to him. Where was the selfish sub when she needed her?

"You…. I didn't…. Let me…."

He smiled and shook his head. "Thank you, but, no. I don't need that tonight. Your pleasure was my pleasure. If you sign the contract tomorrow, we'll seal the deal with a good fuck. How's that?

She nodded, unable to speak.

"Good girl. All I want is for you to be happy."

Oh God. How can I tell him I'm so damned happy I could bust, but at the same time, I want to die?

I can't. I won't. I won't do anything to make him unhappy.

"I'm happy, Master." She smiled to prove it.

Fuck. Fuck. Double fuck. Cluster fuck a duck!

Todd hit the print button and watched in horror as the printer spit out the multi-page contract. He'd meant only to teach Brooke a lesson, but somewhere in the process, she'd gotten under his skin, and like a bad rash, the only way to get rid of her was to wait it out.

He had less than six months to do it, and then he'd be off to whatever team in whatever city would pay the most for his services.

The day before, that had sounded like the best idea he'd ever had, but today he felt like a street corner whore. And it was all because of one unexpectedly addictive sub. Hell, he didn't even know her last name, and she didn't know his. She *wasn't going* to know his.

They'd talked for a while the night before, and he'd learned she owned a successful but demanding specialty bakery in a nearby suburb. She'd barely had time for a social life since the place opened two years ago, which accounted for her rudimentary knowledge of the lifestyle. He'd told her he was a contractor, working for the highest bidder.

It wasn't exactly a lie, but close enough to the truth. He wished she didn't have to work so hard, but long hours in a hot kitchen kept her from keeping up with the news, especially the sports broadcasts. She didn't know who he was, and he wanted to keep it that way. Their relationship was strictly sex and, per the contract he just printed out, to take place within the confines of The Dungeon, where absolutely no one discussed their life outside those walls.

Later, at the clubhouse, he told himself the contract meant nothing. Slipping his jacket off and hanging it in his clubhouse locker, he made sure the envelope containing the document wasn't visible in the breast pocket before he flicked open the cuffs on his dress shirt. He wasn't as careful these days to hide his involvement in the BDSM lifestyle, but he didn't want to explain to anyone, least of all one of the reporters hanging around, that he had a contract of any kind in his pocket.

Contracts. Necessary evils in his profession. The Mustangs had been good to him and paid him well for the years he'd been with them, but all good things had to come to an end. His contract with the Mustangs would expire at the end of the season, as would the one in his pocket. He'd made up his mind to leave, to look somewhere else for whatever it was that was missing in his life.

"Hey."

Todd glanced up from tying his cleats to see Jeff Holder, the Mustangs ace closer, standing over him. "Hey, Jeff. What's up?"

"Not much. What's with the scowl? You got something particular against the Metros?"

"No man, just thinking too hard, I guess." He made a conscious effort to relax his facial muscles.

"You should save that for the game. Don't waste it on tying shoelaces." Jeff clapped him on the shoulder and, with a smile, headed out of the locker room.

Shit. He should be smiling about all the money he was going to make over the next few years instead of scowling. Money would make him happy. A new city, a new team would make him happy.

He stood, automatically reaching for his cap and glove. He scanned the room. Most of his teammates were quietly going about their pregame routines. A few chatted quietly as they changed into their batting practice jerseys. He knew them all, from the veterans to the rookies, he called them friends. They shared more than a love of the game. They had each other's backs. Like the time Tanner lost his house to a brush fire. They'd all pitched in to help him rebuild and replace some of the memorabilia he'd collected over the years.

He was going to miss these guys. They were like family to him.

So why am I leaving? I'll never find this kind of feeling again. No other team will be like this one. Dysfunctional, the lot of them, but good guys with hearts of gold.

Bentley Randolph slapped him on the back with his glove as he passed by on his way out. "Cheer up, man. It's a beautiful day out there."

"Hey, Bent," he said, forcing his lips to curve upward. "Don't get distracted by the birds singing and the pretty, puffy white clouds. We need your full attention in left field."

The outfielder flashed his megawatt smile and took two backward steps toward the door. "Aren't you the funny guy today? I've seen the women who own the block of season tickets above the third-base dugout. The ones that wear the Team Todd T-shirts. You're the one who needs to keep his eyes on the field."

He waved him off. "Yeah, well, you do your job, and I'll do mine."

Randolph gave him a mock salute, turned, and left. Todd grinned all the way to the dugout. They didn't call him Bent for nothing. The guy had a wicked sense of humor he would miss. When things were grim, he could always be relied on to lighten the mood. His fun-loving attitude had lifted the team out of a losing funk into a winning frame of mind on numerous occasions.

He sure hoped his next team had someone like Bent.

Not likely. He's one of a kind.

Todd managed a decent game. He wouldn't make the sports reels tonight, no interviews, but he'd played well. No errors. A single in the third and a ground-rule double in the eighth that should have been a homerun. Probably would have been if he hadn't been thinking about how pretty Brooke's ass was, rosy from those first few swats, instead of focusing on the ball. Next time he put his handprint on her ass, it would be to arouse, not punish.

The thought put a smile on his face that remained there—until later that evening when he pulled into a parking space in the parking garage half a block from The Dungeon. He hadn't offered a woman a contract in years. There simply hadn't been anyone he'd wanted exclusively. A night of pleasure here and there had been enough—up until last night.

He pulled the envelope from his pocket. The document inside was as much for him as it was for her, particularly in regards to the termination clause. He'd modified it to state a specific date when their association would come to an end. It would be a stark reminder to both of them not to look at the months ahead as the beginning of something it could never be.

The impulse the night before to bind her to him forever had been an aberration. Her trust had momentarily blinded him to reality, and holding her afterward had been a huge mistake. One he wouldn't repeat. From now on, he'd make sure she was in a sound frame of mind and body before he left her, but that was all. No cuddling. No talking about…stuff. They didn't need to know anything about each other except how they liked their sex. And he was going to devote the next few months to exploring the subject in depth.

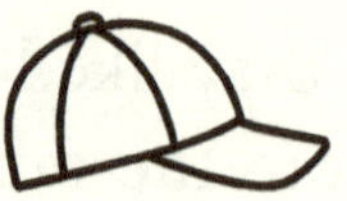

CHAPTER SIX

Brooke looked up from studying the label on her water bottle to see Todd lounging in the doorway. In a room filled with men in leather and women in less-is-more outfits, he stood out in his tailored, navy blue suit and power tie. She imagined him presiding at the head of a table surrounded by lesser mortals, in command without uttering a single word. He was a natural-born leader. It was the way he held himself, as if he knew something no one else in the room did.

She sat straighter, the slight motion drawing his attention to her. Automatically, she moved her hands to her lap and cast her gaze down in deference to his authority over her. They hadn't agreed on terms and hadn't signed a contract yet, but she'd mentally made a commitment, and her body knew it.

He took the chair across from her at the small table she'd claimed in the back of the social area. They would have a measure of privacy to discuss the agreement She had the sudden certainty he knew a lot more about contracts than she did. He probably dealt with complicated business deals daily in his outside life, whereas the only ones she was familiar with consisted of preferences for cake flavors and whether the bride wanted fondant or buttercream frosting.

"I have a contract." He whipped an envelope out of his jacket pocket and slid it across the table to her. "Take your time reading it. Feel free to cross out and initial anything you aren't comfortable with. If there is something you specifically want that I've left out, write it in." A pen joined the envelope on the table.

All business. No wonder he could afford expensively tailored suits. No one in his right mind would dare argue with him when he had that look of complete concentration on his face. He'd be a force to be reckoned with in the boardroom. Or the bedroom.

The thought brought a flush of heat to

her skin. She quickly reached for the envelope, slid the folded contents out, and smoothed them on the table in front of her.

Professional. Concise and well written with headings, subheadings, and bullet points. Either he'd done many of these or he had a secretary who did it for him. Lord, she hoped not. This was too personal for anyone else to see.

"My safe word is soccer?" she asked, latching on to the least personal item of all.

"Do you have something else in mind?"

She shook her head. "No. I wasn't expecting that to be part of the contract. Can I ask why that particular word?"

"It will get my attention." His smile, all playful innocence, lit a fire in her belly.

She had an overwhelming urge to crawl across the table, wrap herself around him, and kiss him. "Oh. You're a soccer fan?" she asked instead.

The smile disappeared, replaced by the stern business face, which held its own appeal. Her heart skipped a beat.

"No personal questions." He gestured to the creased papers. "It's in there."

Sure enough. Section two. Point three.

"No discussion of our lives outside the confines of The Dungeon will be allowed except when pertinent to arranged meeting times or when they might otherwise interfere with the terms of this contract."

"What, exactly, does that mean?"

"My job takes me out of town frequently. It will be necessary at times to discuss travel dates, as they will impact when I can be here for you. You might have late nights or early mornings at work, family obligations. If you have a swim party coming up, you might ask that I not leave any marks that would show when you wear your swimsuit. These are things I need to know."

"Thank you. I appreciate your consideration."

"I'll always take care of you. Sometimes, like last night, it will be necessary to punish you. I don't enjoy leaving those marks, but I do like to see evidence of the pleasure I bring you. Certain marks are meant to be reminders, to extend the pleasure for as long as they last, for you and for me."

Her ass was still pink from his punishment. It didn't take much to leave a mark on her fair skin, and they tended to linger, sometimes for days. "I understand."

She read on. At the end was a list of various types of play with instructions to put a checkmark beside the ones she absolutely did not want to explore. Hard limits. He remained silent while she read, considered, and checked off boxes. When she finished, she was surprised to see how few she had ruled out. She slid the completed forms across the table.

Wringing her hands in her lap, she waited while he flipped through the pages. She hadn't made any changes, but she guessed he wanted to make sure he hadn't missed something. When he got to the last page, he took his time with the list of hard limits. At the end, his gaze moved back up the page to one particular item she had left unchecked.

"You like to be watched?" he asked, one eyebrow elevated.

She shrugged. "I don't know. Maybe. It's a fantasy of mine, you know?" She paused, searching for the right way to express herself.

"I need to know," he said, encouraging her. "I can't make your fantasy come true if you don't clue me in."

"I know. It's just…I don't want just anyone to watch. I want *you* to watch."

"That's why you didn't check off

additional partners."

"It's just a thought. I'm not sure I would want to do it, but I didn't want to mark it as a definite hard limit. Just in case." She was babbling, talking too fast to cover her nervous embarrassment. If she couldn't voice her fantasy to the man she wanted to make it a reality, how on earth could she ever go through with it?

"We'll see. I'm not opposed to the idea. We have a limited time together, and I want to help you explore your limits. See what you're capable of. So, when I'm gone and you seek out another master, you'll have a better understanding of your submissive nature."

"About that," she said. "You're leaving in November?"

"A transfer. I wasn't looking for a long-term relationship. I told you that upfront. I don't know why I'm doing this, but after last night…."

"I know. I felt the same way, too. I want more time with you, sir. If all I have is these next few months with you, then I'll take it."

He spun the papers around to face her, slid them back to her side of the table. Decision time. Six months with Todd as her master. Or nothing. He hadn't said as much, but it was implied. If she didn't sign the contract, he would walk out and she'd probably never see him again.

She picked up the pen and signed her name in the designated spot. He stretched one hand across the table. Brooke placed the pen in his palm. He pulled the papers to him, spun them around. Head bent over the document, he glanced up at her and smiled.

He fixed his signature to the line below hers, folded the papers, and slid them back into the envelope. "I'll bring you a copy next time."

Standing, he tucked the envelope back into his pocket and reached out to her. She allowed him to pull her to her feet.

The top of her head barely came to his shoulder. He exuded power. A shiver, part fear and part exhilaration at having trusted her life to this man, ran through her.

"It's going to be all right. I won't hurt you."

You already have. She kept the thought to herself. She'd agreed to the contract, knowing his leaving would shatter her heart. But that was her problem, not his. She put on her bravest smile and said, "I know."

"Room nine is ours again. I'm going to change into something more suitable, and I'll be there in a few minutes. I don't want to waste a single minute of our time together, so while I change I want you to go to our room, remove your clothes, and wait for me on your knees. Leave the two-way mirror open. We might as well begin working on fulfilling your fantasy tonight."

She was perhaps the strongest woman he'd ever met. She'd been brave enough to confess to her fantasy, and he'd pushed her a step beyond what she had admitted to, telling her to leave the two-way window open. It had been a test, one she passed with flying colors.

Brooke had no idea what she was capable of, but he knew. She had the power to change all his plans. The contract said six months, but if he wasn't careful, he'd be here for a lifetime trying to make her fantasies come true, and that wouldn't do. He deserved some happiness of his own, and a big, fat, eight-figure, seven-year contract would accomplish that. Since the Mustangs couldn't or wouldn't offer him what he wanted, he *would* be leaving. Just not right now.

Six months. He'd teach her what she needed to know about herself as a sub. She'd come out of their liaison in a better position to find a long-term relationship with an experienced master, and he'd enjoy regular gratification for a change.

He'd never wanted exclusivity with a sub, but the idea of this one doing what she'd done to get his attention for anyone else made him caveman crazy. Even letting someone see her like this, naked and vulnerable, was more than he was willing to do yet—no matter he'd promised to test her limits in that regard. He would. Just not today.

Thank goodness the room he'd reserved was at the end of a hallway, so no one had an excuse to go that far down unless they'd been invited. Nevertheless, he'd changed into his leather pants, vest, and boots as if the place was on fire in order to get back and make sure no one was taking an unauthorized peek at what was his.

Mine.

The word felt foreign, but when he said it out loud, "Mine," it tasted sweet. *I've got her.*

So, what am I going to do with her?

"Make her happy," he mumbled to the mirror. "I'm going to make her happy."

She didn't look up when he entered, another giveaway that said she had some experience in the role of a sub. The knowledge both reassured and annoyed him. He stopped in front of her, dropping the bag he'd brought from home at his feet.

"You're beautiful."

Her pert breasts begged for his touch, and since touching them would bring both of them pleasure, he gave in to the impulse, testing their weight and the way their generous size fit the palms of his hands.

"Has anyone ever clamped these?"

"No, sir."

He rolled both nipples between his thumbs and forefingers. Already taut, they grew harder. "Look at me."

She raised her face. Tugging gently on her nipples, he watched her reaction, saw the flush of arousal, the slight flare of her nostrils and softening of her mouth.

"You like that?"

"Yes, sir."

He pinched the tight buds between his

fingers and tugged harder. She inhaled sharply at the initial pain. Her jaw quivered slightly as she absorbed the sensation.

"Good. Very good." He kneeled in front of her and eased the sting by placing his palms flat over the tender skin.

Her gaze automatically dropped.

"Look at me. I didn't tell you otherwise." Once he had her attention, he continued. "We'll start slow with your nipples. Light clamps for a short period of time at first. I'd like to bind your breasts at some point. Perhaps even have your nipples pierced later on. There's a woman who does them here, by appointment."

Todd studied her carefully, watching her face for clues as to how she took the ideas he put forth. She seemed calm enough about the nipple clamps, but when he'd mentioned piercing her nipps, the pulse in her throat spiked.

"Does nipple piercing frighten you?"

"No, sir."

"Your pulse is racing. Why?"

"I...."

"Ah, I understand. It arouses you." He pinched her nipples again, this time adding a twist that startled a groan from her throat. "You like pain. I guess we'll have to see how much."

Once again, he soothed with a firm but undemanding touch. "Last night, the spanking felt good at first, but then you recognized it for what it was. Punishment, not pleasure. There aren't many things I will punish you for, but I will punish you if you break my rules. Do not touch yourself in a sexual way, *ever*, unless I tell you to. Do not flirt with another person, man or woman, unless I tell you to. Do not show your breasts, ass, or pussy to anyone, not even your doctor, unless you seek my permission first. All of those are punishable offenses."

"I understand, sir."

"Good. I promised you a good fuck if you signed the contract. Do you remember?"

"Yes, sir."

"I always fulfill my promises."

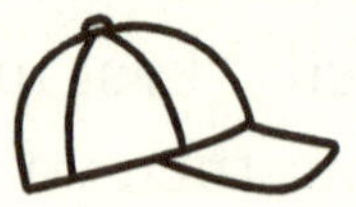

CHAPTER SEVEN

"Whoa! Hold up, Superman!"

Todd slowed his pace, allowing Jason Holder to catch up with him in the hallway leading from the Clubhouse to the dugout. He mentally prepared himself for what was coming. Over the last few months, the pleas for him to stay had become an almost daily annoyance.

"I swear, Holder, the next person to call me that is going to need new teeth."

He resumed walking, and Jason matched his stride. "You can't blame 'em. You've been hitting the cover off the ball. Why don't you share you secret with the rest of us?"

"Here's the secret." He stopped, fisted Jason's jersey in his hand, and drew him close.

He whispered in the younger man's ear. "See the ball. Hit the ball."

Jason smiled and stepped back, raising his hands in surrender when Todd let him go. "Okay, okay. I get the message."

"No, you don't," he said. "The message is, I don't have a clue what I'm doing that's any different than I've been doing for the last ten years. Maybe it's me. Maybe it's the pitchers. Maybe it's the new paint in the clubhouse. All I know is my game is good these days, and I want to keep it that way."

"Whatever it is, we, your humble teammates, are grateful. We just wanted you to know that."

He laughed. "So, you drew the short straw today, huh?"

"Yeah, I did. We want you to stay, man. I'm sure there are lots of teams out there who'll pay you more, but they won't be us. We're special. We loved you even when you couldn't hit for shit. Doesn't that give you a warm, fuzzy feeling?"

"That's the worst please-don't-leave speech I've ever heard."

Jason laughed. "It's true though. Every word. I know warm fuzzy feelings are nothing compared to the heat generated by a fat contract, but as my grandma used to say, 'money isn't everything.'"

"Easy for you to say, Mr. Moneybags," he countered, continuing to the dugout. "I'm looking retirement in the face, and the bigger my nest egg, the bigger my nest."

"Yeah, but just because the egg is big doesn't mean it's good. Think about it, buddy. That's all we're asking."

He thought about what Jason said all through the game. The Mustangs *were* warm and fuzzy, and like an old pair of slippers, they fit just right. They were a great bunch of guys, from the front office all the way to the grounds crew. And they *had* stuck by him on more than one occasion when not only his batting had suffered but his fielding, too. In fact, he'd expected to be traded a few years back, but Doyle Walker had called him into his office, told him to get his shit together— though he'd said it much nicer—even offered to listen to whatever was on Todd's mind if it would help.

He hadn't taken him up on the offer of talking mainly because he wouldn't have had a clue how to tell the team manager his life sucked because he was afraid to date. That had been before Frank Williams had invited him to visit The Dungeon with him and changed his life. He'd found out he wasn't a pervert, and there were plenty of people in the world just like him. He'd also found a safe way to explore his dominant side. He'd found peace.

His game had improved steadily from there, and he was damned grateful the Mustangs hadn't traded him back then. He owed them for that.

And he'd paid them back with six of his best years in the game.

Jason was right, money wasn't everything, but it could buy a shitload of stuff—and peace of mind. That equaled happiness, didn't it?

The truth was, he *did* know what was different.

Brooke.

Since they'd signed their contract, his life had never been better. He smiled more. Laughed more. He looked forward to every home stand because it meant he'd see her again. He'd get to fill himself with her—her scent, the feel of her skin, her laughter, and especially the sounds she made when she came. She was like no other woman he'd ever been with, and despite what the contract said, they'd spent time talking. Mainly, he listened, but he'd told her about his family, leaving off before he mentioned his job.

He didn't know why he withheld the information. It was something he felt he needed to keep to himself, perhaps because doing so would acknowledge what he had with this woman was more than good sex.

It is more than good sex, and you know it.

His new sub was completely open to exploring the deepest recesses of her sexuality, and her trust in him was humbling. She had yet to safe word out of a scene—and he'd taken her to some dark places to which he'd gone right along with her.

Early on, she had expressed a desire to be watched. He'd introduced the possibility the night they signed the contract, asking her to leave the curtain open so anyone who happened by might see her.

Several times since then, he'd arranged for the two-way mirror to be blocked from the outside, blindfolded her, then opened the curtains, planting the idea people were watching her. She'd responded immediately to the imagined stimulus. Tonight, he planned to take it a step further.

Frank Williams was in town. In honor of his induction into the Baseball Hall of Fame, the Mustangs were retiring his number next week, and to celebrate, Todd had invited Frank to The Dungeon for a session with him and Brooke.

Brooke watched through her lashes as her master fastened the leather cuffs to her wrists. He'd seemed in a particularly good mood when he arrived, and for once, he'd opened the curtains over the two-way mirror and hadn't blindfolded her. She was wet just thinking about what his actions meant.

"I've got a surprise for you," he said. "I know how much you like to be watched, so I've arranged for a friend of mine to join us tonight."

Completely disregarding protocol, she jerked her chin up and stared at the mirror. All she saw was the reflection of Todd and herself, but was there someone out there?

"He's there. I wanted a few minutes to prepare you." He lifted one wrist then the other, hooking the cuffs to a bar above her head.

Oh, Lord. Her pulse raced. In order to fasten the cuffs, he had moved to the side, so she was completely exposed to the man behind the mirror. This wasn't hypothetical, was it?

"His name is Frank."

Not hypothetical. The man has a name.

"He taught me everything I know about being a Dom, so no worries there. He's here to observe, but he's an expert with a cat-'o-nine-tails. I've asked him to show me his technique again."

He knelt, fixed cuffs around her ankles, and attached a spreader bar between them. She couldn't quit staring at the mirror. Her nipples grew hard, and her pussy tingled at the thought of being watched and flogged by another Dom.

"I wouldn't let him touch you if I didn't trust him." He straightened, moving to stand directly in front of her, so she had no choice but to look at him. His hands skimmed along her sides, from her armpits to her hips then up again to cup her breasts. "You're beautiful."

She lifted her chin, needing to see what was in his eyes. Amusement. Excitement. Lust. She forgot they were being observed and fell under the spell of his gaze.

"I've been dreaming of this for weeks." He bent his head and took her lips in a rare kiss that made her knees weak and her pussy ache.

She let her wrists and the bar take more of her weight, the bite of pain a reminder of her situation.

"I had to taste your lips before I taste the rest of you." He reached for something in his back pocket. "You'll need this."

A ball gag dangled from his fingertips.

"Don't worry," he said, inserting the ball between her lips. "I have a handkerchief for you." He produced a square of white cloth and pressed it into her right hand. "If you need us to stop, drop the handkerchief."

He stepped away, leaving her completely exposed and vulnerable. Her gaze darted to the mirror then back to the man restraining her.

"I'm going to let him in," he said, his gaze intent on her face.

She let her eyes speak for her, showing him all the trust and faith she had in him.

The door swung wide. Frank stood in the opening, taking her naked body in with assessing eyes. Cool air from the hallway gave her gooseflesh and caused her nipples to tighten, but he made no attempt to shut the door.

This room was in a busy part of the club. What if someone walked by?

"She's beautiful. It's almost a shame to keep her behind a closed door," he said.

Heat warmed her from the inside out. Frank was older than her master, but not by much. He had the look of a businessman who took care of himself, from his muscled legs encased in black leather to the smooth, carved musculature of his bare chest. In one hand, he held a flogger, the nine knotted leather strands dangling along the length of his right leg.

"Close the door, Frank. This is a private session," Todd said.

"Whatever you say." Frank stepped into the room, closing the door behind him. He came to stand in front of her, his gaze still examining her in detail. She hadn't thought her nipples could get any harder, but when he looked directly at them, the painful tightening made her eyes water.

"Brooke, this is my friend, Frank. Frank, Brooke." Todd made the unnecessary introductions then moved to the mirror, pulling the curtains closed, sealing her inside with two very experienced Doms. She drew a deep breath through her nostrils and let it out.

"I'm at your service," Frank bowed to her.

She inclined her head in acknowledgment of the older man.

"We're here for you, babe. Your master assures me you need and want to feel the flogger. He also tells me it is your wish to be observed by a third party."

She nodded, and Todd approached. Frank moved away, allowing him access. He smiled at her, lifted her left breast in his right hand. Bending, he took her nipple in his mouth and sucked hard. She closed her eyes, groaning at the sensation of wet heat, the tugging that seemed as if her nipple was connected to her pussy.

The air shifted around her, and she opened her eyes to see Frank staring at her. Their gazes locked, held for a heat-charged moment. Then Frank broke away, his gaze traveling to her breast and the man suckling there.

Lust filled Frank's gaze, and something in her soared. Todd moved to her other breast, lavished attention on it then, with his hands at her waist, moved lower. The top of his head descended until it stopped level with her mound. The first flick of his tongue over her clit had her rocking her hips, begging for more.

Frank stepped closer. She looked away from Todd and the delicious things he was doing between her legs. Her gaze locked with Frank's, and she couldn't look away. It was undoubtedly the most erotic moments of her life, looking into the bottomless eyes of one man, seeing the lust there, while another man drove her insane with his lips and tongue.

She struggled against her restraints, wanting desperately to touch, to have reassuring human contact. But she was on her own, locked away from what she needed from one man and locked in to the fiery gaze of another.

Her chest heaved with the effort to take in enough air through her nostrils. Sounds of longing, of desire, of intense pleasure formed only to be swallowed by the gag. Reduced to her eyes for communication she used them to beg.

He must have seen her cry for help. Frank moved to her side, their gazes locked in silent understanding. He raised the flogger to her chest, dangled the thin leather strips over her aching nipples, letting the hard knots knock against her distended flesh.

"You need to come, don't you?" he asked, his voice low, seductive, knowing.

She let her eyes speak for her.

Slowly, he moved to stand behind her. He pressed himself against her, his erection digging into the small of her back. The flogger dangled over her shoulder, keeping up the rhythmic teasing of her nipples. His other hand wrapped around her forehead, applying pressure until the back of her head rested against his shoulder. He stroked her brow, along her temple to her jaw. His fingers traced her thinned lips, over her chin, and down the length of her neck.

"You're beautiful like this, at our mercy. We know how to make you feel good."

He flicked the hard handle of the flogger against her right nipple a few times then came back harder.

She struggled against him, but Frank held her tight, allowing her little range of motion. The pain dulled quickly, but the heightened sensation in that breast was matched by an answering sensation low in her belly. He flicked the handle over her left nipple. This time, she was ready for the sharp bite when the handle came down hard on her sensitized flesh.

"You're doing great," Frank crooned in her ear. "Just a little more, and we'll let you come."

Holding her head steady, her neck exposed, he trailed tiny bites from her jaw to her collarbone, punctuating each one with words she could hardly comprehend.

"I like seeing his head between your legs. I can smell your arousal, hear him slurping up your juices. You're so damned beautiful. He wanted so badly to show you off. Now, I see why."

She closed her eyes, the sensations taking over. Two mouths devoured her, the firm presence of Todd's wide shoulders between her thighs, the solid presence of the other Dom at her back, the unyielding restraints at her wrists and ankles. It was a potent combination that robbed her of inhibition. Having this man, this stranger to her, watch…. It was beyond anything she had ever imagined.

"Look at him," Frank commanded, using his hand to force her chin to her chest. "Watch him eat your cunt. You do this to him. He'll do anything to make you happy, even share you with a man like me. You like this don't you? You like having me watch you."

She did. Oh, Christ, she did. The gag captured her moan. She was so close to coming, but she didn't have permission to. She closed her eyes in an effort to stave off the inevitable. She was going to come without her master's consent.

"Eyes open," Frank growled. His hand at her nape insured she could see only what he wanted her to see. He brought the flogger across her body, the strands brushing the top of Todd's head. The handle, held horizontal, brushed over both nipples then he brought it hard against her breasts, mashing both flat under the leather-wrapped grip.

Pain blinded her. She fought for breath and for sanity.

"Use the pain." Frank pressed still harder against her tender flesh.

Her nostrils flared in short, staccato bursts with each hard-won breath.

"Center it where it belongs. Use it," he repeated. "Come for him. Come for me."

Todd licked her slit, invaded her with his tongue. She couldn't hold it back. The orgasm assaulted her body with hard waves of pleasure fed by the pain in her breasts and the certainty this kind of pleasure was worth any amount of punishment she might have to endure for having taken it without permission. She closed her eyes, seeing in her mind what she couldn't see through the blinding pleasure/pain—the self-satisfied smile her master always wore after he made her lose control. The image increased her gratification because pleasing him was the greatest pleasure of all.

The crashing waves gentled to soft rolls, and she realized the pain at her breasts had subsided, and her head was once again cradled against Frank's shoulder. His cheek was pressed against her temple, his hand stroking her brow in tandem with his reassuring words.

"You're safe, darlin'. Let it come. Give it all to us. That's it, baby. Breathe."

Tears streamed from her closed lids. Todd continued to stroke her pussy with his tongue, loving her instead of trying to arouse. He was always so careful with her, taking her to heights she never fathomed she could reach, then tenderly caring for her until she drifted back down.

Love for him filled her heart and warmed her all the way to her soul. Half their time together was gone, and as the days ticked away, she was more and more certain there would never be another man for her. She would allow him to share her with men he trusted, but when he moved on, he would take her heart, her desire with him.

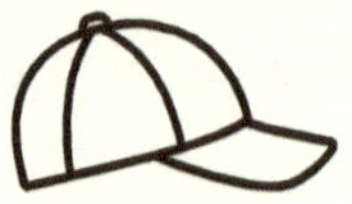

CHAPTER EIGHT

Todd lay in bed, watching the single band of sunlight peeking through the curtains creep farther up the opposite wall. It was a good thing the Mustangs had a day off because he was in no condition to play.

Physically, he was sound. It was the non-physical that wasn't cooperating. The previous night with Brooke and Frank had blown his mind. Her first orgasm would have brought him to his knees if he hadn't already been there, but her second had done something to him he couldn't explain.

As her master, he'd known she would do well with Frank watching, and as he'd anticipated, Frank hadn't sat on the sidelines. He'd been a full participant, using his immense knowledge of women to increase her pleasure tenfold. But after she'd come down, Frank had started in on her with that wicked flogger of his, taking her back up to the pinnacle. Todd had watched as each strike of leather, expertly applied, left her skin layered with red striations, and through it all, she'd never taken her eyes off him.

She'd looked at him—*to* him—the entire time. Without the ball gag she'd worn during the first session, she could have said anything, but she hadn't made a peep until Frank slapped her cunt, wrapping the knotted leather from her mound to her ass. She'd spoken one word, "Master."

The single utterance had been a plea for permission to come, which he'd granted with a nod of his head. Frank administered another slap to her pussy, and she'd given in, accepting the pleasure until it had rendered her as limp as a rag doll.

Her gaze had held him captive, silently telling him she understood. He had invited Frank to join them as much to fulfill her fantasy as to fulfill his own. He'd wanted to watch her with another man.

Her second orgasm and, later, the

blowjob she'd given Frank had been gifts for him.

No other sub had ever known him that well. He'd never allowed one to know him that well.

Dust motes swirled in the light that had changed from a soft gold to bright white. In a few short weeks, his professional and personal contracts would expire. He would be a free agent, able to choose to play for and with anyone he wanted.

What do you want?

He propped up against the headboard and let the question sink in.

I want to be happy.

What makes you happy?

"Brooke. Brooke makes me happy."

He laughed out loud. All the money in the world couldn't match the way he'd felt the night before just being with a woman who gave everything to him.

Todd swung his feet to the floor, simultaneously reaching for his cell phone. He opened the drapes and looked out at his perfectly landscaped backyard while he made the necessary phone calls.

His agent wasn't happy, but he'd perked

up when Todd had given him the go-ahead to shop endorsement deals—if he was able to convince the Mustangs to keep him.

His palms were sweating, for Christ's sake! Todd wiped them on his pants then adjusted his tie. Jeans were his usual off-day wardrobe, but he figured if he was going to beg, it might go over better if he looked serious.

He couldn't be more serious. If the Mustangs weren't interested in keeping him, he didn't know what he would do. Retire, probably. There was one thing he knew for sure, he wasn't ready to leave Brooke. She had a successful business to run, and it wouldn't be fair to ask her to walk away from it to follow him God knew where. He needed to stay in Dallas.

Maybe things wouldn't work out with her, but he owed it to both of them to give it more time. If that meant taking less money and a shorter contract, or Heaven forbid, retiring, then that was what he would do.

Walker's secretary waved him on in. "He's expecting you," she said with a smile.

He wished he knew what kind of smile it was—a nice knowing you smile, or relax, it's going to be okay, smile. Cynthia knew everything that went on in the organization, sometimes before anyone else did. Maybe he should ask *her* about his contract—save himself the trouble of taking back his own words.

"Thanks."

When Todd entered, Doyle stood.

"Stevens. What brings you here on your day off?" He gestured to a seating area that boasted a sofa and a couple of armchairs grouped around a coffee table.

Todd chose the sofa, and the Mustangs' manager sat in one of the chairs. He swiped his hands on his thighs, deciding there was no sense beating around the proverbial bush.

"I've changed my mind about leaving. If the Mustangs are still offering a five-year contract at the rate we discussed earlier in the year, I'll sign." He hoped the desperation he felt inside wasn't evident in his voice. At least he hadn't said he'd sign anything in order to stay. He hadn't sunk that low. Yet.

Doyle turned his head toward the plate-glass window spanning the back wall of his office and overlooking the playing field below.

He was quiet so long Todd began counting his heartbeats just to make sure he was still alive. The fact the answer wasn't an automatic no gave him hope.

Doyle spoke to the window. "Do you want to tell me why you've changed your mind?"

Not really. He hedged. "Several of the players have asked me to stay."

Turning back to face him, it was clear Doyle wasn't buying his explanation "Okay, so you don't want to tell me, but before I go back to the head office with this, I have to know. Will we get one hundred percent from you for the life of the contract, or will you be wishing you'd jumped the fence?"

"I'll give the Mustangs one hundred percent. If I thought I wasn't capable of that, I wouldn't ask you to keep me on."

Doyle nodded, his gaze searching Todd's face. The man was good at reading people. He refused to look away, letting the older man see his sincerity.

"I'll call you." Doyle stood, and he followed the manager's lead. "I don't expect there will be a problem, but don't take your house off the market yet."

"I never put it on the market," he said. And if that wasn't a sign he never wanted to go in the first place, he didn't know what was.

Patience was something Todd usually had plenty of. He made his living waiting for the right pitch and watching for gaps in the other team's defense. The trait carried over to his private life as well. Taking the time to build a sub's orgasm, one thin layer of sensation at a time, never failed to pay off in the end.

Waiting to hear from the Mustangs regarding his contract felt like a slow-motion ride through hell. But underneath the hellish uncertainty was a layer of peace he gripped tighter than a baseball bat. No matter what the team's decision, he would be happy with it. For the first time in his life, baseball was just a game. It was an odd feeling seeing the sport he had loved since he was five years old and swung his first real bat at a real ball on a tee, from a different perspective.

Baseball had ruled his life for almost three decades. When he'd turned nine, his entire family had moved, so he could play in the best Little League organization in the area. He'd chosen his high school based on their baseball program and sought out the most competitive of traveling teams in the off-seasons. Baseball had paid his way through college and, as a pro, given him the means to do as he pleased.

He would give the Mustangs one hundred percent on the field if they chose to keep him, but for once, baseball didn't seem like the most important thing in his life. He'd made the mistake of letting the game hold that position for too long, and like every other workaholic, it had cost him his happiness.

Never again. Brooke had shown him the source of his unhappiness, and he owed it to both of them to see if what they had together was enough for a lifetime.

Brooke's pulse raced as it always did when her master arrived. She tracked his movements with lowered eyes. He wore the black leather pants she loved so much. His feet were bare, and probably his chest, too, but she couldn't quite see that high unless she cheated and peeked when he turned his back. He always smelled so good, like summer grass with citrus undertones. She'd committed his scent along with so many other details, to memory, knowing the day would come soon when he would leave.

The unwelcome reminder of the finite nature of their relationship made her reckless. She didn't want to be punished, but anything was worth the risk if it added to her store of memories.

He turned, and the grating sound the zipper on the bag he carried his 'toys' in filled the room. Her gaze darted up the length of his legs to his firm ass, then beyond to the broad expanse of his back—gloriously nude. Her inner camera captured the line of each sculpted muscle, layering the image with stored tactile recollections to create a three-D memory.

"Did I tell you to look at me?" he asked, swiveling at the waist. His gaze locked on hers, and she swallowed hard.

"No, sir. I'm sorry. I…."

"You what?" he asked, returning to stand before her.

He towered over her on her knees, but

she wasn't afraid. He might choose to punish her for breaking protocol, but he would never hurt her.

"I just wanted to look at you, sir."

He crouched in front of her. Amusement lifted the corners of the lips she loved so much. "And why would you want to do that? You've seen me plenty of times."

"Permission to speak frankly, sir?"

"Granted."

"I don't want to forget you. When this is over."

His smile faded, and her heart dropped to her toes. They hadn't discussed the rapidly approaching end of their contract, and clearly bringing it up had been a bad idea.

He stood, paced a few steps away, and returned to stand over her. "Do you want this to come to an end?"

"No, sir. I wish it didn't have to. I don't want you to go."

"If I didn't leave, would that make you happy?"

"Yes, sir." She'd already walked out on the limb, might as well tell him everything. "I want to be with you…for as long as you will have me…sir."

Silence, broken only by his slow inhale and exhale, filled the room. She wished she knew where he was getting the air. To her, it seemed as if her words had sucked all the oxygen out of the room. Her head spun, and an overwhelming urge to run out of the room, naked or not, consumed her. Nothing could be as bad as waiting for him to respond.

"We need to talk," he said, startling her lungs into functioning again. "Stand up."

He placed a hand beneath her elbow to help her stand. Once she was on her feet, he guided her to the platform bed and motioned for her to sit on the edge. He joined her, hunched over, his forearms braced on his thighs.

"I'd like to tear up our contract," he said.

She froze from the inside out. Why had she told him the truth? He'd said from the beginning it couldn't be permanent, and she had agreed to the terms. Her impulsive words were going to cost her what little time she had left with him. A lump of ice blocked her throat, froze her vocal cords, and freeze-dried her tears. She couldn't even protest his statement!

A full-body shiver gripped her, and she shook like a dry leaf in the wind.

"Shit. You're cold." He jumped up, grabbed a blanket from the stack on the counter, and draped it over her shoulders. His touch was gentle, his concern for her well-being a reminder of why she didn't want him to go. "I'm sorry, babe. I thought it was warm enough in here for you."

He rose again, this time to adjust the thermostat. Clutching the blanket around her with stiff fingers, she prayed he would get this over with quickly and leave before she shattered. Already, she could feel the cracks forming in her icy shell.

"That should help," he said, returning to sit beside her.

He wrapped his arms around her and pulled her against his chest. Her head fit perfectly beneath his chin. Eventually, her tremors eased, and he set her away. She'd thawed enough to allow a tear to escape and slip down her cheek. He wiped it away with his thumb.

"Hey. Why are you crying?"

He wanted to tear up their contract, so basically, she was no longer his sub. She looked him in the eye, his equal. "I don't want you to tear up the contract. Please, Todd, sir." *Old habits die hard.*

The idiot smiled, and she discovered anger could thaw a solid block of ice.

"Don't you dare laugh at me. You're the one who wants out, not me. We both signed that contract, so we both should have to agree to tear it up."

"I agree," he said, his smile growing wider. "What if I can convince you to tear it up?"

"You can't." She sounded like a pouting child, but she couldn't help it. Her heart practically had a calendar pinned on it with a big red X marking the date it would break. Today was not that day. She felt cheated and...*used.* "The contract gives you rights but not that one."

"Actually, I think it does, but that's beside the point. Will you calm down and listen for a minute? I think I can convince you tearing up the contract is in your best interest."

"Go ahead. Talk." *But I don't have to listen.*

She shifted so he was looking at the back of her head. He startled her by placing his hands on her shoulders and leaning in.

His lips brushed her ear. "I'm not leaving."

His hot breath against her skin rattled her senses. Had she heard correctly? Something that felt a little like hope blossomed in her chest and stole the air from her lungs.

"What?" she gasped.

"I'm staying right here," he clarified.

His tongue traced the shell of her ear. She shivered again, but this time it had nothing to do with being cold.

"Tear up the contract. I don't want an expiration date on the way I feel when I'm with you."

Heat incinerated the sinister calendar on her heart, counting down the days to self-destruct. "You're staying?"

"I'm staying. At least five years. Longer if this thing works out with us." He nuzzled her neck, her ear, her cheek. "I want us to have all the time in the world to see if what we have between us can last." He turned her, pressed her flat on the mattress, and covered her with his big, hard body. "Will you tear up the contract?"

His smile was gone. She'd never seen him look so vulnerable as if his happiness depended on her answer. There was much she didn't know about this man, but she knew everything that counted. He was dependable and strong. He had a good heart, and though he ruled over her, he didn't abuse his power. He gave more than he took.

"We'll write a new one with no end date if you're worried about the specifics, but I would never hurt you. You have to know that by now."

She did know that about him, too. Her safety had always come first, even when she had been far less inclined to worry about such things. He'd rather stop short of his goals than harm her.

"I know." She smiled up at him. "I know everything about you I need to know. Do you think five years will be enough?"

"I don't think it will take that long because I think I'm falling in love with you and I don't want any timeframe on letting that happen."

He parted the blanket, found her hands, and brought them up over her head. He used his legs to bring her fully beneath him on the mattress and laced his fingers with hers so they were palm to palm, their bodies touching at all the key points—hands, chests, abdomen.

His erection felt like a torch burning

through his pants, branding her.

"Say something," he pleaded. "I'm dying here."

Worry lines creased his forehead and carved a deep groove between his eyes. It was tempting to make him wait, something he was all too fond of doing to her. *I've wanted to say these words for so long. I can't keep him waiting any longer.*

"I'm falling in love with you, too," she said. "If I agree to tear up the contract, will you make love to me?"

A wide smile worked like a magic wand, eliminating worry lines and bringing a sparkle to his eyes. He rocked his hips against her, demanding entrance. She parted her legs, inviting him to take her.

As quickly as it had come, his smile disappeared, replaced by a soft determination. "I'm going to make love to you all night," he promised.

She smiled up at the man who held her heart. "Is that paper I hear tearing?"

Todd thrust deep. Wet heat wrapped around his cock, held his flesh prisoner. He'd always understood the D/s power exchange on an intellectual level, but until he met Brooke, he hadn't truly understood the submissive partner held as much power—perhaps more—than the dominant one. His body was enslaved to this woman, his physical pleasure contingent on hers. Yet, tied as he was to her, he'd never felt as free as he did when he was with her.

Her needs were the answer to his needs. Her desires a perfect match to his. He'd thought happiness was measured in dollars, but thanks to this special woman, he now knew it was measured in degrees of trust.

And by trusting everything she was to him, she'd made him the happiest man on Earth.

ABOUT THE AUTHOR

USA Today Best-Selling author Roz Lee is the author of over thirty romances. The first, The Lust Boat, was born of an idea acquired while on a Caribbean cruise with her family and soon blossomed into a five-book series initially published by Red Sage. Following her love of baseball, Roz turned her attention to sexy athletes in tight pants, writing the critically acclaimed Mustangs Baseball series.

Roz has been married to her best friend, and high school sweetheart, for over four decades. They have two daughters and are the proud grandparents of three adorable grandkids. Roz and her husband live in the wilds of New Jersey with their Labrador Retriever, Bud which is code for Big Unruly Dog.

Even though Roz has lived on both coasts, her heart lies in between, in Texas. A Texan by birth, she can trace her family back to the Republic of Texas. With roots that deep, she says, "You can't ever really leave."

When Roz isn't writing, she's reading or traipsing around the country on one adventure or another. No trip is too small, no tourist trap too cheesy, and no road unworthy of travel.